LITTLE BOAT

Thomas Docherty

templar books
an imprint of Candlewick Press

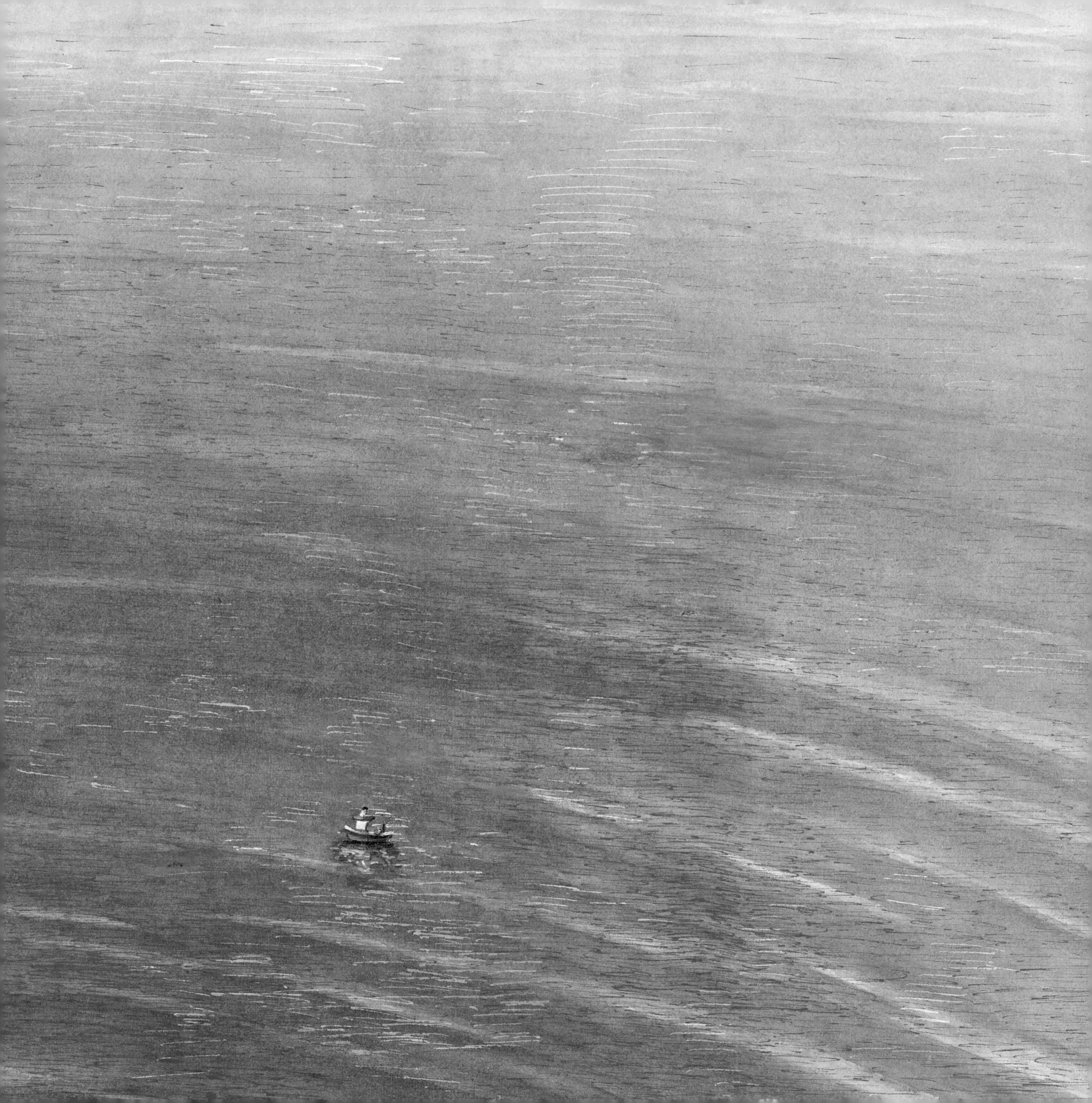

The ocean is a big place, and I am just a little boat.

But I chart my own course

and I drop my own anchor.

The sea is always changing and full of dangers,

but I sail on . . .

through terrible storms . . .

up and down

rolling waves . . .

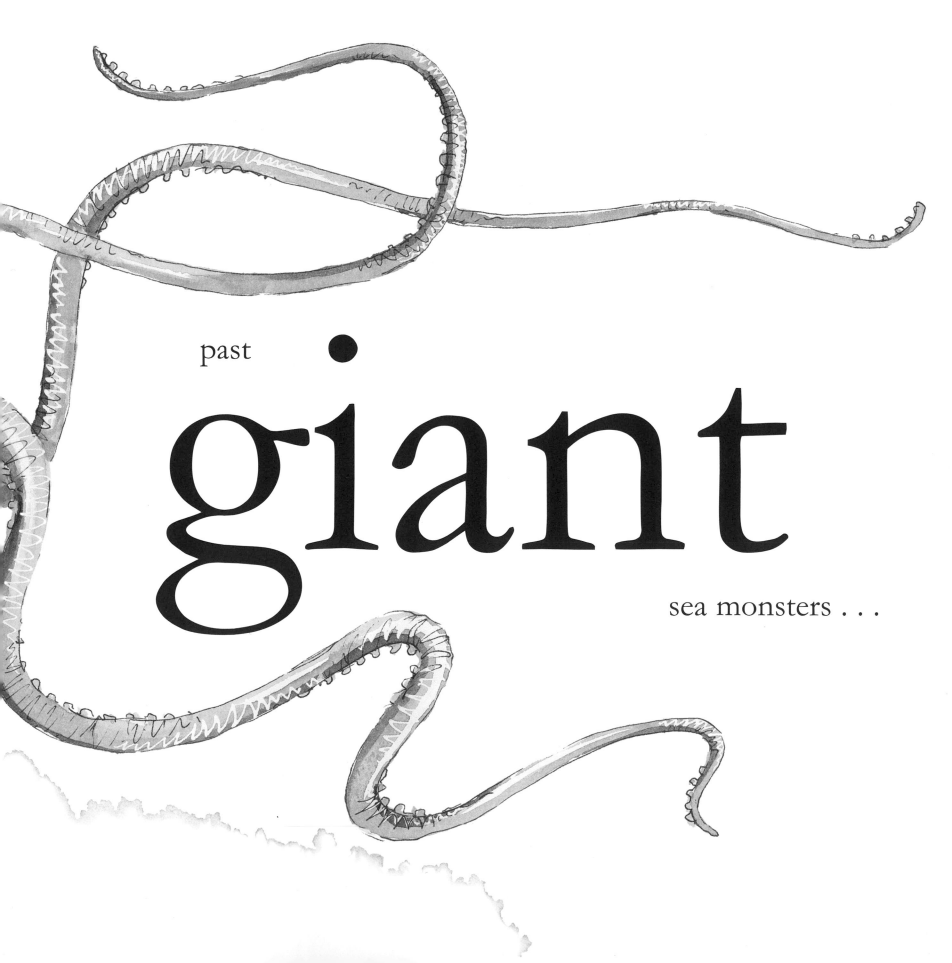

past **giant** sea monsters . . .

and around treacherous rocks,

in search of · · ·

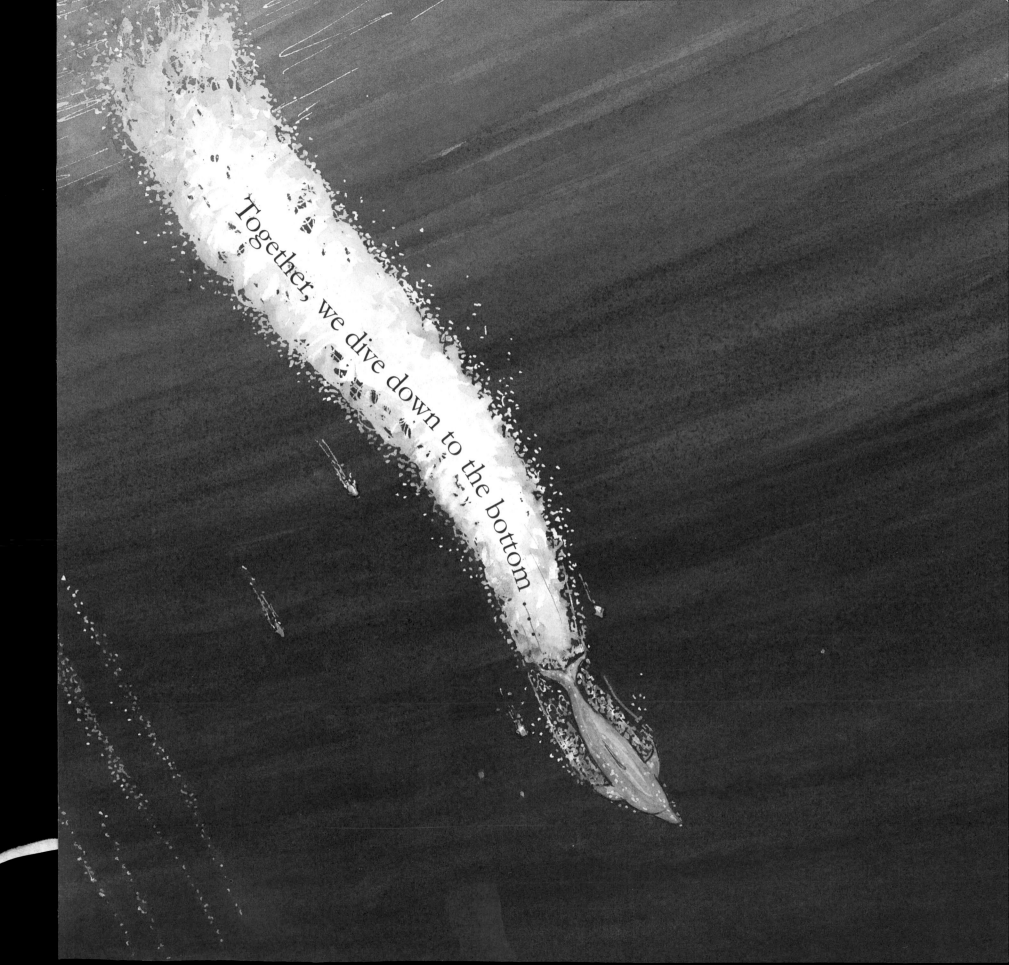

Together, we dive down to the bottom

and climb up to the top.

We go round and round in circles . . .

and never want to stop.

Full steam ahead to the edge of the world . . .

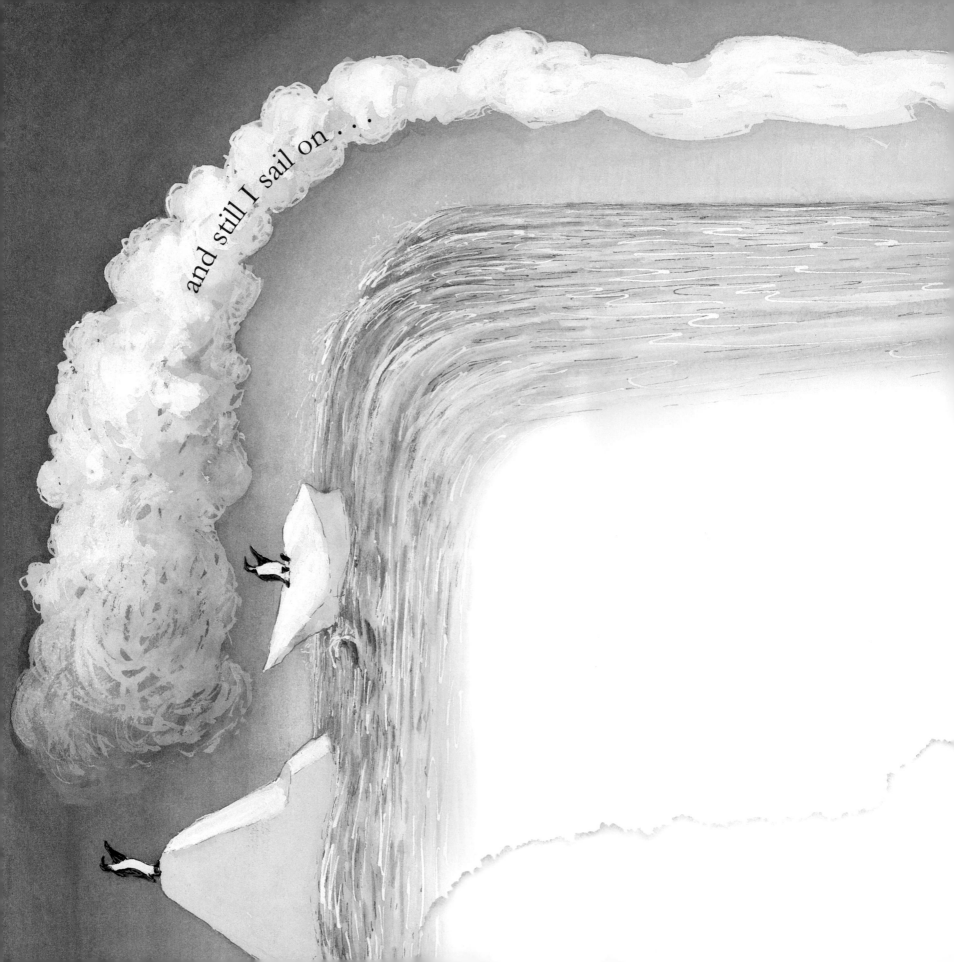

and still I sail on . . . .

because now no ocean is too big . . .

for a little boat like me.

 – T. D.

First U.S. edition 2009

Library of Congress Cataloging-in-Publication Data is available.
Library of Congress Catalog Card Number 2008935297.
ISBN 978-0-7636-4428-4

10 9 8 7 6 5 4 3 2 1

Printed in China

This book was typeset in Garamond.
The illustrations were done in watercolor and ink on paper.

A TEMPLAR BOOK

An imprint of
Candlewick Press
99 Dover Street
Somerville, Massachusetts 02144
www.candlewick.com